To Ann and Ray, my sweet parents!
—M.P.

A portion of the money you pay for this book goes to Sesame Workshop. It is put right back into
"Sesame Street" and other Sesame Workshop educational projects. Thanks for helping!

Library of Congress Cataloging-in-Publication Data: Pantuso, Mike. Food! by Cookie Monster / illustrated
by Mike Pantuso. p. cm. SUMMARY: Cookie Monster describes some of the foods he likes to eat.
ISBN 0-375-81391-8 [1. Food—Fiction. 2. Food habits—Fiction. 3. Puppets—Fiction.]
I. Title. PZ7.P1937 Fo 2002 [E]—dc21 00-069834
www.randomhouse.com/kids/sesame   www.sesamestreet.com
Printed in Mexico June 2002 10 9 8 7 6 5 4 3 2 1

FOOD! by Cookie Monster

Illustrated by Mike Pantuso

Random House 🏠 New York

FOOD!
Dee-licious!

Me love

healthy food!

Happy yummy
birthday!

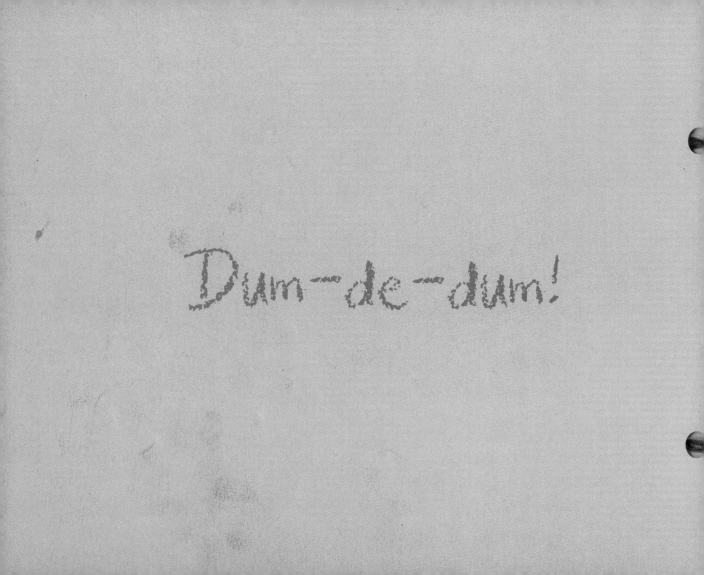

Dum—de—dum!

cereal

Rice

Snack time—
Cookie's
favorite time!

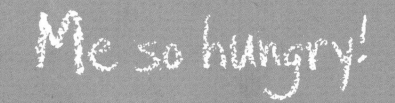
Me so hungry!

Good movie.
Great popcorn!

Happy
turkey day!

Sand-wiches.
Yummy!

Me love to eat

COOKIES!!!

Mike Pantuso, the artist who helped Cookie Monster make the drawings in this book, is the senior graphic designer for *Sesame Street*. He's been collaborating with the residents of Sesame Street since 1987, bringing their storybooks, paintings, and artistic ideas to life. He lives in New York City and Doylestown, Pennsylvania, with his wife and daughter, a cat, and an iguana.